D1577111

WHAT HAPPENED?

LAB MICE HEIST

Book design by Jake Slavik
Illustrations by Courtney Huddleston

Design Elements: Shutterstock Images

Published in the United States by Jolly Fish Press, an imprint of North Star Editions, Inc.

First Edition
First Printing, 2019

This is a work of fiction. Names, characters, places, and incidents are either the product of the author's imagination or are used fictitiously, and any resemblance to actual persons living or dead, business establishments, events, or locales is entirely coincidental.

Library of Congress Cataloging-in-Publication Data
Names: Weaver, Verity, author. | Huddleston, Courtney, illustrator.
Title: Lab mice heist / by Verity Weaver ; illustrated by Courtney Huddleston.
Description: First edition. | Mendota Heights, MN : Jolly Fish Press, [2020] | Series: What happened? | Summary: "The lab mice from Ms. Abaza's fifth grade science class have disappeared, and each student has his or her own theory about what happened to them"—Provided by publisher.
Identifiers: LCCN 2019001866 (print) | LCCN 2019004534 (ebook) | ISBN 9781631633096 (ebook) | ISBN 9781631633089 (pbk.) | ISBN 9781631633072 (hardcover)
Subjects: | CYAC: Mice—Fiction. | Lost and found possessions—Fiction. | Schools—Fiction. | LCGFT: Fiction.
Classification: LCC PZ7.1.W41777 (ebook) | LCC PZ7.1.W41777 Lab 2019 (print) | DDC [Fic]—dc23
LC record available at https://lccn.loc.gov/2019001866

Jolly Fish Press
North Star Editions, Inc.
2297 Waters Drive
Mendota Heights, MN 55120
www.jollyfishpress.com

Printed in the United States of America

WHAT HAPPENED?

LAB MICE HEIST

by VERITY WEAVER

illustrated by COURTNEY HUDDLESTON

text by KATE GORDON

JOLLY
FiSH
PRESS

Mendota Heights, Minnesota

Chapter 1

MOUSE-NAPPED!

Monday, March 3, 8:45 a.m.

"Whoa. What do you think is in that?" whispered Jeremiah.

Ms. Abaza had arrived in the fifth-grade classroom, carrying a big cardboard box.

Everyone in the class was thinking the same thing. Ms. Abaza was a really exciting teacher. She often brought in strange and wonderful things to show the class, or she took them to visit amazing places. One year, she took her whole class to climb a mountain! But that's another story. Today, the strange and wonderful thing arrived in the form of a big cardboard box.

And everybody was super curious about what was inside.

"Maybe it's a cake?" asked Tom hopefully. "Or a big box of Pop-Tarts, with enough for all of us!" He sat up taller in his seat to see.

Behind him, Mara groaned and leaned back in her seat. Tom

was tall enough as it was, and now she could barely see anything over his shiny blond hair.

"Don't be silly," said Yolanda, rolling her eyes behind her thick-framed glasses. "Pop-Tarts are only for breakfast."

"Not for me, they're not," said Tom. He held on to his rumbling belly.

The class erupted into animated, curious whispers. The only person who didn't join in was Jedda. She was new in class and still a bit too shy to share her opinions with her classmates. She shook her curly brown-and-gold hair so it hung further over her face, picked up her marker, and made a start on her biology project.

The rest of the class grew louder and louder.

"Children!" Ms. Abaza said, holding up her hands for quiet. As she did so, her phone dropped from the pocket of her colorful dress.

Jeremiah rushed to retrieve the phone. As he did so, he tried to take a sneaky peek in Ms. Abaza's box. It was no good. There was no way to see what was inside. But he did notice that he could hear a faint scuffling noise . . .

"Thank you, Jeremiah," Ms. Abaza said, smiling. "Back to your seat now."

Mara wrinkled her nose. "Ew. I can smell something coming from the box. It smells like pee." She pulled out a bottle of bubble-gum-scented body spray and spritzed it in the air. She was trying to be sneaky about it, but the whole room suddenly filled with bubble-gum scent, as if it had been transformed into a candy store.

"Maybe it is," said Ms. Abaza, laughing. Her big dark eyes twinkled. She put the box down on her desk, adjusted her embroidered pink hijab, and turned to the class with one eyebrow raised. "And please put down the spray bottle, Mara. I'm pretty sure what I have in the box isn't a fan of bubble gum."

"Does pee like bubble gum?" asked Mara, looking confused. She took hold of one of her long red pigtails and began twirling it around her finger, an annoyed expression on her face. "Wait, so you're saying it's *not* pee? Because pee doesn't, like, like *anything*, right?"

Ms. Abaza shook her head at Mara and moved over to the whiteboard. She drew a circle with some lines coming from its sides. Then she drew something beneath the circle that looked almost like . . . a mouth? And then . . . yes! Those were definitely paws! And a belly and back and big, round ears! Finally, she drew a long tail that looked like a worm.

"That looks just like Peter Pack Rat!" Yolanda said. When her classmates looked at her blankly, she added, "From the old Atari game? Oh my gosh, you guys are more clueless than a Magikarp who never gets to be a Gyarados." While they just continued staring blankly, Yolanda looked hopefully at Ms. Abaza. "Is it a vintage Atari? Please let it be a vintage Atari. Or any other kind of gaming console would be fine . . ."

"Sorry, Yolanda," Ms. Abaza said pleasantly.

Yolanda sighed and dropped her chin to her hand. How was she ever going to become the best girl coder in the United States if she had to do all her gaming research outside of school?

"But you're close," Ms. Abaza went on. "I'm a really terrible artist, it's true, but what's in the box *is* very close to a rat."

She opened the box and lifted a small cage with a handle. The lid was made of blue plastic. The cage had see-through sides that she kept hidden behind the cardboard box. Ms. Abaza waited for a moment while the kids sat up higher in their chairs, craning to see inside.

"Be very quiet," Ms. Abaza said, holding a finger to her lips. "They don't like loud noises."

For a moment, a little bud of hope blossomed in Jedda's chest. When she was little, she'd had a tiny blue-tongued skink that she had kept as a pet. His name was Irwin, and he had a carrier just like that one when he was small. Maybe there was a blue-tongued skink in the cage, like Irwin! Jedda thought she might feel less homesick, if there was . . .

But then she remembered. There were no blue-tongued skinks in the United States—just like there were no episodes of *Saddle Club* or Vegemite.

Ms. Abaza slowly lifted the cage for everyone to see.

Five tiny little mice sat in a huddle in one corner, nestled in paper. Two of them were plain white. One was white and brown and spotty. Another was half white and half brown, and the fifth was completely brown. They all had teeny, tiny pink paws and long, thin wormlike tails. They looked up at the students with wide, curious eyes. They seemed to be watching the students, waiting to see what the students would do.

The students stared at the mice. They remembered what Ms. Abaza had said about being silent, but it was so hard to hold in their excitement.

Finally, Tom couldn't hold it in any longer. "Awesome," he said quietly, looking around the room and grinning at his friends.

"We get mice!" Yolanda whispered, pumping the air with her fist. This was even better than an Atari! She'd always wanted a pet mouse, but her mom said their cat, Hulk, would eat it for breakfast.

That was probably true. He once chewed up Yolanda's shoelaces for breakfast.

The mice responded to the noises by making noises of their own—little squeaks and scuffling sounds in the ripped-up paper in the corner of their cage. On the other side of the cage, there was a bowl filled with pellets and small dried peas. There was a water bottle hanging from one wall, a fluffy hammock for the mice to sleep in, and a small plastic wheel. The bottom of the cage was covered in paper.

"Are they ours to keep?" Tom asked. "Mice are awesome!"

Jeremiah was the first one to approach the desk. He loved animals, and he'd handled mice before—his therapist had some in her office. She said that her patients found them calming. Jeremiah often felt the exact opposite of calm, but never around animals.

On his way to the desk, he tied back his black braids with a scrunchie, so the beads wouldn't clatter and frighten the mice.

"I love them," he whispered.

"Can we all come up?" asked Yolanda.

"If you're quiet," said Ms. Abaza. She removed the lid of the cage so the kids could look down inside. "Remember, this is new for them. They might be feeling a bit scared."

"I'm not coming up," Mara said, crossing her arms. "They're gross. And I don't want to end up smelling like pee."

"Fine," said Yolanda breezily. "More room for the rest of us to see."

Mara just *hmphed* and looked away.

Jeremiah peered into the cage, where the mice were still huddled in a corner. "Are you sure they're okay in there?" he asked. "They don't look very happy. And the cage is very small. I feel like they want to be free."

"They're very happy," Ms. Abaza assured him. "And we will be letting them out of the cage sometimes, when they're more used to us."

"I totally want to code some sort of obstacle course for them to run through," Yolanda said, bouncing on her heels. She pushed up the sleeves on her vintage Super Mario hoodie and gestured excitedly, demonstrating her plan. "We could have robot spheres dart randomly in front of the mice, like *ninjas*, so the mice have to figure out—"

"Nah," Tom said. "I'm going to teach them to play soccer. With teeny, tiny balls."

Jedda didn't say anything, but she loved watching the mice. She hoped they started to get more comfortable with the students soon. Jedda knew what it was like to be in a new place and feel lonely and scared. When she'd first arrived at Checkerbloom Elementary, the other kids had wanted to talk to her and ask her questions all the time. She knew they were just curious about her, but it had still made her feel really anxious. A lot of them were surprised when she said she was an Aboriginal Australian—a Palawa from Tasmania. Some of them had never even heard of Tasmania! It was nice that they were so interested in her, but when they crowded around her, she wished she could just run away.

Often, at lunchtime, instead of sitting with the other kids, she climbed the big oak tree at the edge of the sports field and hid up there for the whole lunch break, so she wouldn't have to talk to any of the other kids. She felt that, if the mice had an oak tree to climb, they'd be climbing it now.

"I'm going to call them Ronaldo, Beckham, Messi, Maradona, and Owen," said Tom, "after famous soccer players."

"No way!" Yolanda cried. "They should totally be Ada,

Shafi, Anita, Betty, and Éva, after famous women in computer programming!"

From the back of the classroom, Mara piped up. "I think they should be called Stinky, Smelly, Filthy, Dirty, and Mr. Pee."

The other students rolled their eyes.

"Mara, mice actually aren't all that smelly," Jeremiah pointed out. "Not if you take care of them properly."

"Whatever. I'm not touching them," Mara said crossly. "I just hope their stink doesn't waft over to me and make me smell like mouse."

"That won't happen, Mara," Ms. Abaza said calmly, "and how about we name our new pets tomorrow?" She smiled at the kids. "For the rest of today, we're just going to let them settle in and get used to their surroundings."

Some of the kids grumbled. They wanted to play with their new class pets *now*!

"Don't worry," Ms. Abaza said. "There will be plenty of time for us to hang out with these little guys. They're not going anywhere for a while. After recess, we've got plenty more to look forward to, including doing some cool experiments with fizzy soda!" She closed the lid of the cage.

Jeremiah noticed that she forgot to fit the lid properly, so he did it for her.

The rest of the day passed quickly, as days always did in Ms.

Abaza's classroom. The fizzy soda experiments were fun (and sticky!), and in the afternoon, students read to each other from some funny books. Yolanda laughed so much at a joke Tom read her ("What do you call a fake noodle? Impasta!") that she cried. Before the kids knew it, the bell was ringing. It was time to go home! The kids scrambled for their bags.

Tom scooped up his soccer bag—he was off to practice before he headed home. As he passed Mara's desk, she snapped, "What's in the bag, Starlet? It smells worse than the mice."

Tom looked down at his bag and avoided Mara's eyes.

Yolanda overheard them and wondered why Mara had called Tom "Starlet." Mara had said it in a way that sounded mean . . . Then again, Mara said most things in a way that sounded mean. Yolanda remembered that Tom used to have a picture on his locker of some old-fashioned movie star. She wondered if that had something to do with it. Weird.

Yolanda grabbed her gaming backpack and new wireless headphones. One of her moms was picking her up from school. She'd want to *talk* the whole way home about "important things," so Yolanda wanted to listen to some of her favorite gaming podcast until her mom arrived. She grinned at Jeremiah as she passed him, but he didn't seem to notice her. He was too busy arranging his messenger bag.

Jeremiah got his things together slowly and carefully,

arranging his books next to each other with great care. He liked the way the edges lined up perfectly. He liked the way his shiny pencil case fit on top. It always made him feel more in control if he did things methodically. He looked over at Jedda when he was done. She was going slowly too. He wondered if she felt the same way he did about making sure everything was in order. He wondered, for a second, if he should wait for her and walk out with her, but he was trying to be more punctual lately. He didn't want to take too long getting home. He gave her a little wave as he passed her, and she waved back shyly.

Jedda didn't go slowly to feel calm. She liked being the last one out of the classroom. It meant she didn't have to talk to the other kids by the lockers. She waited until Jeremiah was done—fiddling about with items on her desk and doodling in her notebook to pass the time—before she picked up the backpack her auntie had given her before Jedda had left Australia. Finally, when the noises outside the classroom quieted a bit, she stood and moved toward the door.

Tuesday, March 4, 8:33 a.m.

The next day, the kids got to the classroom earlier than usual, eagerly discussing the mice out in the hallway. The only one who wasn't with them was Mara.

"Maybe she took the day off, to recover from the mouse

fumes," Yolanda joked. She put on a fancy English accent. "A day in bed, with a prescription of ten squirts of body spray per hour, and she'll be back to tip-top health."

After a few minutes of chatting, the ten-minute warning bell rang.

Yolanda called out, "You ready to go in, Class of Awesome? It's mouse o'clock!"

The students entered the classroom, still arguing over what the mice should be called.

"One should definitely be called Bruno Mars," Jeremiah was saying. "And the others—hey!" He pointed at the cage, still sitting on Ms. Abaza's desk.

The kids ran over to look inside. It was empty!

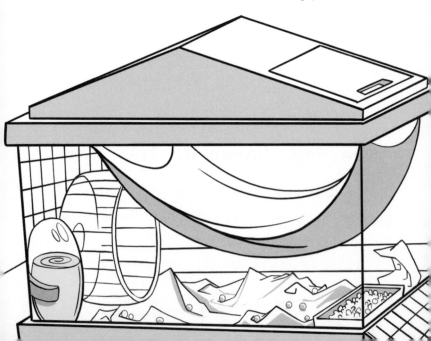

"Oh no!" Yolanda gasped, running her hand through her short black hair. "What happened?"

"This is . . . not good," said Tom.

"What are we going to do?" asked Jeremiah.

A thick blueberry scent wafted through the classroom door.

"What's going on?" said Mara, stopping in the doorway.

Jedda finally found her voice. "It's the mice! The mice are gone!"

Chapter 2

Tom, Tuesday, March 4, 8:20 a.m.

"It's way too early to be awake," Chloe says grouchily. Chloe is my little sister. She's eight, and she hates mornings. For most of her life, she's a bundle of sunshine, but before 9:00 a.m.? She's a tsunami of crankiness.

We're on our way to school. Checkerbloom Elementary—where we both go—is only five minutes' walk from our house. As soon as I turned ten, Mom said it would be okay for us to walk to school without her, so long as I was a grown-up and took good care of Chloe.

Most days, we eat breakfast before we go, but today it was so hard getting Chloe out of bed that we're eating on the run. Chloe is eating cereal straight from the box, without any milk or anything, which I think is straight-up gross. I, of course, am eating Pop-Tarts: Brown Sugar Cinnamon, unfrosted. The classic kind of Pop-Tart. The polar opposite of straight-up gross.

On the sidewalk, a little finch sings a happy morning song.

"Be quiet, bird!" Chloe says angrily.

"Hey!" I say. "I know what will cheer you up. I was going to tell you last night, but you were out late at your book club—"

"Wait. I said 'hi' when I got in."

"I know. But I was busy watching my movie."

"Oh my gosh—someone call the newspapers. Tom watched a *movie*. That *never* happens." Chloe puts on a super pretend-astonished face.

"Put a sock in it, Sarcastic Sally, or I won't tell you the cool thing."

Chloe mimes putting a sock in her mouth, then grins at me.

"Better. Okay, the cool thing is . . . we got mice!"

Chloe's grin sags like a leaky balloon. "Like, in our house? Are you kidding? They better not chew on any of my Percy Jackson books."

"No, dork. At school. We got class mice. They're awesome. I mean, they will be, once we're allowed to play with them and stuff. We haven't even named the mice yet. Yesterday, they mostly slept."

"Duh. Mice are totally nocturnal." Chloe says it through a mouthful of cereal, spraying crumbs everywhere. "I read it in a book."

"Call the newspapers!" I roll my eyes.

She winks, and I laugh. I know a bunch of people who really hate their brothers and sisters. But Chloe's rad—brave, clever, and funny. Even if she does have her nose stuck in a book so often that I'm sometimes tempted to squish her nose *in* the book.

I'm so lucky to have a kid sister like Chloe. After 9:00 a.m., of course.

When we get to the school gates, Chloe punches me on the arm. "Later, bro," she says before running off to join her friends. They're standing in a circle, comparing library books. They're all total nerds, but I think it's awesome they all have something they're passionate about. It's like me and old movies. I know, I know—everybody thinks it's soccer I'm obsessed with. But I'm not really. I mean, soccer's fun, but I want to be a movie critic someday.

I don't tell many people that. It might seem weird—someone like me wanting to be a *critic*. I mean, I'm a pretty easygoing sort of guy, and I don't actually *like* being too critical in regular life. But as soon as a movie comes on . . .

Well, I have been known to yell at the TV, is all I'm saying. In movies, I expect *perfection*. When I'm watching movies, it's like all the things I *don't* feel in regular life, I suddenly feel 500 percent.

I see some of the guys from soccer on the way in to school. We chat about Los Angeles FC's chances in this weekend's El Tráfico match against the Galaxy. (Slim to none, I'm hoping).

After a few minutes, I wave goodbye to my teammates and race up the stairs toward the lockers. I have a bunch of soccer stickers on the front of mine, of course. I used to have a really small picture of Audrey Hepburn too. She's an awesome old-timey movie star I really love. But Mara kept making jokes about it, so I had to take it down.

I still have pictures hidden inside my locker though. I have Marilyn Monroe and Grace Kelly. And Audrey, of course. It's safe to have them in there. Nobody can see them in there.

Mara is kind of my enemy, I guess. When I first started here at Checkerbloom, she seemed okay. She wore cool dresses and big bright-pink bows in her hair. She was also super quiet, which was okay by me—I'm pretty quiet, too, most of the time.

But then suddenly, one summer, she got a mean streak. She stopped being so quiet and started talking *lots*—which would have been fine, but some of the stuff she said was really mean and sarcastic. She was especially mean to Jeremiah, and he got upset because they had been good friends. I told her that she shouldn't treat people that way, and she got really angry and started being super mean to me too.

I hear her coming before I see her. She has these clippy-cloppy platform sandals that make a loud noise. They're the first thing you notice. Then there's the smell. She has this habit of spraying body spray all over herself, *all* the time. It smells good—like candy and cake and stuff—and I'd think it was a funny habit, except it's Mara, so I hate it.

Today, she smells like blueberries, and she's running, for some reason. We're not allowed to run in the hallways.

I turn to see her approaching. Her long red hair is flying behind her, almost like a superhero cape. It would look cool. If it wasn't *her*.

"What are you staring at, Starlet?" she asks, slowing to a halt in front of my locker and clutching a glittery handbag to her chest.

That's the other thing—the other reason Mara McCullough and I are enemies. After she noticed the little Audrey Hepburn picture, she started calling me "Starlet." She says it like it's a bad thing or a rude word. I don't actually mind the word, but I do mind it when she says it in front of my teammates. They don't think old movies are cool, like I do. They only like movies about sports and funny cartoons.

"Just wondering where you're going in such a hurry," I say.

I might be imagining it, but I'm sure I see her skin turn paler behind her freckles.

"None of your b-beeswax," she hisses.

Her green eyes flash with anger. She reminds me of the snake, Kaa, in *The Jungle Book* movie. Except she doesn't have those super swirly eyes. And, in fact, she looks a bit nervous.

Her eyes flick past me, so she's looking inside my locker. She starts to smirk a bit.

"Oh, Starlet," she says. "Look at all those pretty photos. You do know there have been movies since the nineteenth century?"

I bite my tongue, trying so hard not to tell her that the first ever movie wasn't even produced until 1888, right at the *end* of the nineteenth century. She is not worthy of that knowledge.

She winks at me. "Gotta go," she says.

And I'm mad because I can't think of anything to say to her. There are no words inside my head.

Not even "bumbershoot" or "nincompoop" or "catawampus," all of which Chloe sometimes whispers in my ear to make me laugh. She loves big, strange words—the funnier-sounding, the better.

But right now, nothing feels funny.

I shove my books into my locker.

I keep my math book and my class novel, because I'll need

those for the start of the day. Unless Ms. Abaza decides to do something unexpected and amazing, which she sometimes does. One day, we took a field trip to the beach and spent the whole day digging for fossils! Another day, she took us all down to the cafeteria and gave us a bunch of premade cakes and candy and icing and told us we had one hour to decorate the cakes. Whoever made the most amazing cake won a prize. (Jeremiah won. His cake looked like a castle—it was *incredible*.) And yesterday . . .

Yesterday, she brought in mice!

Suddenly, I feel a bit better. I'd almost forgotten about the mice. I'm so excited to see them again and convince my classmates to give them soccer names!

"Hey, Tom!"

I turn around to see Yolanda rushing toward me. I give her a big smile. Yolanda is really cool. Today, she's wearing an awesome red sweater that says, "Cool Girls Code."

"Hey, Yolanda!" I say. "Excited to see the mice?"

"Totally," she says, grinning. "They are my muses. I'm turning them into a video game."

"Of course you are." I smile.

She does a little bounce. "It's going to be epic—sort of *Sonic the Hedgehog* meets *Zelda*, with mice with magical powers and super speed and an evil robot bad guy who flies in a zeppelin. You know what a zeppelin is? It's like an old-timey flying ship

from the Victorian era that looks a bit like a foot-long sandwich but, like, without salami or anything. I'm going to make it all set in the Victorian era, I think, and use lots of steam-powered stuff. Oh, and maybe I could . . ."

I let her keep talking, and I half listen, smiling to myself. It's cool, listening to someone talk about something they're really excited about.

"Anyway, so I totally want to watch the mice *all day* today, so I can observe their behavior and take notes and use my observations to make my game mice as realistic as possible. What do you think?"

"I think that your game sounds awesome," I say, grinning up at her. "I mean . . . *cool*? And that's not *code* for something else."

She tilts her head to one side, eyes narrowed. She reminds me of a computer that's loading.

"Uh-huh," she says finally. "Because of my T-shirt. Completely terrible joke, Tom. Did your dad teach you that one?"

I feel really awkward for a second, but then she grins and adds, "Oh, who am I kidding? Any joke about coding gets five stars from me."

We walk together to the classroom door. It's always unlocked when we get there, but we have this habit of catching up for a few minutes in the hall before we go in. It's kind of like our morning party, but without the streamers and balloons. I greet some of my other classmates. Everyone seems excited and happy. It makes me feel happy too. I feel especially happy because Mara isn't here yet. But then I wonder, where was she rushing off to anyway?

I notice Jedda, our exchange student, standing by herself. I'm feeling pretty happy after Yolanda liked my joke, so I try another one. "Hey, Jedda," I say. "What flies around the school at night? The alpha-bat!"

She just blinks at me and looks down at her shoes.

I hope that doesn't mean she doesn't like me. I think she's cool. I love her hair, and I think it's fascinating that she's from Australia. Nicole Kidman is from Australia, and I *love* her! When Jedda first started here a few weeks ago, I was going to ask her if she knew Nicole Kidman, but Chloe told me not to be a dork. But she did ask me if I could ask Jedda about whether they have yetis in Australia, and whether Vegemite really tastes like feet.

It's almost time to go in, but Mara still isn't here.

"Maybe she took the day off, to recover from the mouse fumes," Yolanda says, before making a joke in a bad British accent.

I'm about to tell her that I saw Mara in the hall (leaving out the part where she was mean about my locker photos), but then Yolanda goes off to chat to Jeremiah about something, so I don't get a chance to.

When the warning bell rings, Yolanda calls out, "You ready to go in, Class of Awesome? It's mouse o'clock!"

We walk into the classroom, still chatting and laughing.

Jeremiah is the first one to notice that the mice have disappeared.

Chapter 3

Tom, Tuesday, March 4, 8:37 a.m.

I finally think of something to say to Mara.

And it isn't "bumbershoot" or "nincompoop" or "catawampus" (or "flibbertigibbet" or "lackadaisical").

"You did it, didn't you?" I say, pointing at her.

Her pale cheeks turn bright pink. "What do you mean, Tom?" she asks. I must have flustered her—she totally forgot to call me "Starlet."

"You set the mice free!"

Mara gasps, her palms pressed to her cheeks.

"What are you talking about, Tom?" asks Yolanda.

"Yeah," says Jeremiah. "You can't just say that. You can't accuse someone of something without evidence."

I want to remind him how mean Mara is to him—how she stares at him and laughs when he says stuff that isn't even funny. I want to tell him he shouldn't be defending her.

Instead, I say, "I do have evidence. Or, at least, I have some stuff that *might* be evidence. But maybe we should wait 'til Ms. Abaza gets here, before we—"

"And what if Ms. Abaza has been kidnapped by the same people who kidnapped—I mean, *mouse*-napped—the mice?" Yolanda raises her eyebrows. "Not that I'm saying that's what's happened. Mouse-napping, I mean. But if that's the case, we need to solve this right now."

"I didn't kidnap Ms. Abaza!" Mara squeaks. "I don't even know how to do a k-kidnapping! I mean, I guess I could google it, but—"

"I'm not saying you kidnapped Ms. Abaza," I say quickly. "And we have no way of knowing if she was kidnapped at all. I mean, it seems unlikely, but I've seen enough movies to know that *anything's* possible. I do have evidence that Mara took the mice though!"

"Let's hear him out," says Yolanda warily. "Just while we wait for Ms. Abaza." She side-eyes Mara, and I realize that maybe she's not Mara's biggest fan either. "I mean until we get Ms. Abaza's ransom note, of course. Then all bets are off."

"Let's hear *both* of them out," says Jedda quietly.

I glance over at her. She gives me a small smile. (Inside, I do a happy dance. Maybe she doesn't hate me after all?)

"It's always important to hear both sides of a story," she adds with a shrug. "That's what my dad always says anyway."

"There is no story!" Mara cries. "I mean . . . who says *anyone* let the mice out? And why do you think it's me? I wouldn't even know *how* to google about mouse-napping. I don't think there are even websites about that!"

"Let's listen to Tom," says Yolanda. "Then we'll listen to you." She turns to me. "Tom? You have a good reason for accusing Mara, don't you?"

"He'd better," Mara grumbles. She flounces over to her desk and flops down in her seat, her arms crossed and her chin jutting out.

I narrow my eyes at her. If Mara was in a movie, I'd be giving her performance right now one Pop-Tart, which is my own unique way of rating movies.

The thought makes me feel better. Less weird about talking to everyone. If I pretend this is a movie . . . I can sort of sit outside it, and maybe it won't feel so nerve-wracking.

The rest of my classmates go to their desks, leaving me standing at the front. It feels like I'm standing in the spotlight. Like I'm the star of the show. Which is *weird*. I never feel like that, not even on the soccer field. I'm always just part of the team. I'm usually just a regular member of this class too—sort of a jock, sort of smart, sort of funny, sort of quiet, sort of just . . . normal. Nobody ever stares right at me, like everyone is now.

If I was in a movie, I'd be singing a show-stopping number right now.

I am not in a movie.

But if I was . . . if life was one big musical and I *could* break into song?

What rhymes with Mara?

Carbonara?

Sayonara?

Capybara . . .

"Tom?" Yolanda's voice brings me back from Hollywood to the real world and my classroom, where everyone is still staring at me.

I know I can't break into song. And I don't really want to. I'm a *critic*, not an actor, after all. But rating Mara before definitely helped calm my nerves. Maybe I could . . . keep doing that?

I'd give Yolanda five Pop-Tarts right now. She's smiling at me in a super supportive way. She deserves *all* the Pop-Tarts.

"Right," I say. "Mice. So, here's what happened—"

"What *you* think happened," Jeremiah corrects me.

Two Pop-Tarts.

"What *didn't* happen!" Mara cries. She slams her hand down on her desk. Her eyes are shining. "You know *nothing*, Tom Roe," she mutters.

I could almost give her a high rating for acting so angry and innocent when she is clearly guilty, but . . . nope.

No Pop-Tarts. One big bowl of week-old, moldy brussels sprouts.

I hold up my hands. Everyone goes quiet. I feel powerful, like how I imagine movie stars must feel every day.

"What happened to our laboratory mice is this . . ."

I can't make it a song, but I can make it an awesome monologue. I imagine I'm in a courtroom scene. I might not be the best actor in the world, but I have watched enough movies to know the basics of creating drama.

I put one hand in the pocket of my jeans, imagining that, instead, I'm wearing a lawyer's pinstriped suit. I take some paper from Ms. Abaza's desk to use as a prop, imagining I'm holding an important court document. And . . . I begin.

"You heard Mara say yesterday how smelly and gross the mice are. You heard her say that she was worried that the mouse

stink would waft over to her. And I can kind of understand why Mara was worried about that. She really likes nice smells, which I think is awesome—"

I didn't mean to say that bit, and I'm kind of surprised at myself. I thought I hated Mara's perfumes, but . . . they're actually pretty nice. Especially the one that I think is meant to smell like cupcakes (but smells to me exactly like Pop-Tarts).

"Anyway, she was worried about the mouse smell," I add quickly.

"That is not evidence," Mara says. "That's, like, completely unrelated to anything. That's not *my motivation*."

Moldy sprouts.

"She's right," Jeremiah says. "You've gotta have more than that."

Not moldy sprouts but definitely no Pop-Tarts.

I catch Mara sneaking a look at Jeremiah. For once, it doesn't seem mocking or mean. She looks grateful and almost . . . happy?

She *almost* smiles at him in a way that looks *friendly*.

But that can't be right. Mara doesn't like anyone. Mara thinks she's *better* than everyone. Especially me, Jeremiah, *and* the stinky mice.

"I do have more than that," I say.

Mara is now frowning at me so hard there's a big crease in the middle of her forehead, like the crack between the sections of a Kit Kat bar. I kind of feel bad, because she looks so worried, but . . .

What's most important is that we find our mice. And if Mara did mouse-nap the mice, then she might be able to help us get them back.

I take a deep breath and continue my prosecution.

"She was in a hurry to get somewhere this morning. Or *away* from somewhere. I don't know. Maybe she had already mouse-napped the mice, and she was running away from the scene of the crime. Like, probably, that's what was happening. If this was a movie, that would be the case, anyway . . ."

I trail off. I meet Mara's eyes, and I guess I'm waiting for her to deny it or get mad.

But she doesn't.

Instead, she does the last thing I would have ever expected (like, I would be less surprised if Pop-Tarts started suddenly tasting like bugs).

Instead of arguing with me, Mara starts to cry.

I never make people cry. Not even Chloe, and she deserves it sometimes. (She may be the best sister in the whole world, but she's still a younger sister, and sometimes, she puts slime in my hair while I'm sleeping.) I probably shouldn't care so much, because Mara has made more than a few people in our class cry (including me, the day she made fun of my Audrey picture), but it just feels *bad*.

I give myself two bowls of moldy sprouts.

"I'm sorry, Mara," I say. "Even if you did let the mice out, it's okay. We can still catch them. We can fix this. Don't cry, please."

"They're . . . not . . . that . . . s-stinky," Mara says. She squeezes her eyes closed, shaking her head. "I didn't even think they were that stinky! I would never let the mice out because they were stinky! You're so *mean,* Tom!"

Now I feel really terrible. Because it doesn't look like she's lying. It looks like she's telling the truth.

If I accused Mara of something she didn't do and I made her cry . . . that makes me just as bad as she is, doesn't it?

"I'm really sorry," I say again, dropping the paper and my act.

Jedda gets up from her seat and goes over to Mara. She puts her arm around Mara's shoulder. "You know," she says, "where I come from, we have a native kind of mouse, called a long-tailed mouse. They're really ace. They can hop! And they're really brave and resilient. Even when there's heaps of logging in their habitat, they somehow seem to survive. *But* they do eat moss and bugs and fungi, mostly, so I reckon they'd have *really* stinky breath."

She puts her hands up in front of her collarbone, like two little paws, and pulls her lips back over her teeth. "Feed me fungus!"

she says in a little squeaky Australian mouse voice. She sounds just like Nicole Kidman, if Nicole Kidman was a mouse.

It makes Mara laugh.

It makes me like Jedda even more. She's awesome. *ALL THE POP-TARTS.*

I'm glad she cheered Mara up. But I still feel bad that I made Mara feel sad. And, also, if it's true that Mara *didn't* mouse-nap the mice, then . . . where did they go?

Did they just escape by themselves? (In which case, maybe we should give them all names of famous escape artists, instead of soccer players.)

Or did someone *else* mouse-nap them?

"Well . . . if Mara didn't do it," Yolanda says, as if she's reading my mind, "then . . . I have an idea of what might have happened."

Everyone turns away from me to look at Yolanda. And I don't mind at all.

"And yes," Yolanda goes on, "we should probably wait for Ms. Abaza before we go all James Bond on this—although, wouldn't it be awesome if we could suddenly have rocket packs and phone watches and—"

"Yolanda, what do you think happened?" Jeremiah interrupts.

Yolanda closes her mouth quickly. She hesitates, like she's reconsidering speaking up. But then she leaps up from her seat and joins me at the front of the class. I'm about to slink away, like a ninja, but Yolanda grabs my arm, squeezes it, and winks.

She whispers in my ear, "It's okay. You made a mistake. It happens. Even in the movies."

All the Pop-Tarts. Brown sugar ones.

I realize then that maybe Yolanda knows how much I secretly love movies. Maybe that's not a bad thing at all. I look around the class. Nobody (except Mara) is giving me mean looks. Nobody (except Mara) seems mad at me. Mara looks like she wants to dangle me by the toes over a pool full of piranhas.

But everyone else has moved on. They're just wrapped up in the mystery. What's going to happen next?

If this was a movie, I'd give it four Pop-Tarts so far. But I need to see what happens in the ending before I lock that rating in.

Now everyone is looking at Yolanda. Everyone is waiting for Yolanda to tell them what really happened in the *Lab Mice Heist*.

Chapter 4

Yolanda, Tuesday, March 4, 8:20 a.m.

"Did you remember to pack your gym shoes? You forgot last week, remember, and I had to drop them off, which was absolutely fine, darling, but I have a meeting today, so I just wanted to make sure you had them. And I put three pieces of fruit in your lunch box today, because yesterday, you only ate your crackers and your sandwich, and you even took your pickle out of your sandwich, and I'm worried you're going to get scurvy if you don't start eating some fruits and vegetables, and I *know* Mom only cooked you mac and cheese for dinner last night. So just eat your apple and your banana at least, okay, darling? And don't forget you have that English homework due tomorrow, and I know you didn't do it last night, because you were busy doing your new game design, so maybe get a start at lunchtime, okay? And remember . . ."

I am so tempted to put on my headphones. It's Mamá's turn to walk me to school this morning, and it was her turn to pick me up yesterday. Which means I get back-to-back Mamá, which means back-to-back questions.

Yesterday, it was all, "Who did you play with today, darling?" (As if I'm still four years old and spent the day building with Tinkertoys. Which, actually, would be kinda awesome . . .)

And, "Did you eat your grapes at lunch?" (I lied, obviously. Grapes are pretty much eyeballs with seeds.)

Today, I'm getting so many reminders. *So. Many. Reminders.* My brain is so full of reminders they might start marching out of my nostrils.

Which I would tell Mamá, except then she'd go all Super Worried Mamá about it and try and suggest I go see the school psychologist to free up some more brain room or something.

I miss Mom walking me to school. When Mom walks me to school, she lets me listen to music, or she tells me about the art projects she's working on. (Right now, she's working on an enormous gnu made entirely of glue bottles—it's a glue gnu!) She only asks me questions if I seem upset.

Don't get me wrong—I love both my mothers equally. But Mamá can just be so full-on sometimes.

Mamá finally takes a breath, and I seize the opportunity to change the subject.

"Hey, so, did you wanna hear about my game?" I ask her.

Mamá blinks at me for a moment, clearly trying to work out whether she should call me out for interrupting her or whether she should transform into Super Supportive Mamá and listen to what I have to say. Obviously, one of her child psychology books told her that listening to your kids is "very important for their development," so she smiles and says, "Sure, darling. What's it about?"

"Well . . ." I tell her all about my game. I'm thinking of calling it *Micescapades*, and it'll be sort of *Sonic* meets *Zelda*, with superpowered mice but steampunk (kind of like *Hugo* or *The Golden Compass*). It's going to be totally GOAT (Greatest Of All Time)!

Mamá tries her best to seem interested, but she doesn't really understand gaming. When she was my age, they didn't even have the internet at home. *I know, right?*

Caveman times.

Anyway, it's fine. Mom is a big gamer—she's a bit younger

than Mamá. But Mamá is great in lots of different ways. She's a really amazing writer, and she is super connected to our Mexican heritage, and she makes the best hojarascas in the whole of California—maybe even the world! I will hunt down anyone who says otherwise and feed them grapes.

Plus, Mamá loves me "more than chocolate," she says, which is kind of a big deal for someone who loves sweet things as much as she does. She says I am her best and sweetest creation. *Aw* . . .

So even if it was Mom's belly that I lived in (though I'm made from Mamá's egg—it's complicated), I love both my mothers just the same.

At the school gates, Mamá gives me a big hug and a sticky kiss on my forehead.

"Hasta luego, bomboncita," she says to me, which means "See you later, sweetie" in Spanish.

"Adiós, Mamá!" I say.

As I'm heading toward the school entrance (I want to grab a coding book from the library to help with some complicated stuff in my new game), I see Jeremiah walking through the parking lot. Mamá is heading in that direction, and I hear her say, "Hola!" to him as he rushes by.

Jeremiah doesn't say, "Hola!" back. He doesn't even seem to notice her.

This is not *completely* weird. Jeremiah is often in his own little world. I almost always see him walking to school with headphones in, but he's not wearing headphones right now.

What's weirder is that he's here this early. I'm almost always here a bit early, whether it's because I have coding club, or I want to use the library, or one of my mothers has somewhere to be (or just because I really want to get away from Mamá's questions).

But Jeremiah is never here early.

I once heard him say to Tom that he likes chatting with the birds on his way to school. He keeps his headphones on and sings to them and tells them stuff he doesn't tell anyone else.

Mara was also eavesdropping on their conversation, and when Jeremiah said the thing about talking to birds, she told him it was "totally weird and bizarre." But I thought it was super cool. In fact, I wrote a note in my journal of game design ideas to make a character one day who talks and sings to birds. Maybe not in the mouse game though. Birds might try to eat a mouse. No mice-eating birds in my game. Maybe bird-eating mice though. Maybe *zombie* bird-eating mice.

My point is . . . Jeremiah is often tardy. So why is he here at this time today?

Weird.

I let Jeremiah continue on his way to the playground. I know how super focused he gets, and I don't want to interrupt him if he's in the middle of some Important Thinking Time. I keep walking toward the school entrance.

That's when I see her. *Mara.*

She's standing behind a tree, like she's trying to hide, except with hair as bright as hers (and a candy-pink polka-dotted sweater *and* a glittery handbag), there's no missing her.

She's watching Jeremiah.

I get this kind of barfy feeling in my stomach when I see her watching him. Like, maybe she's planning a prank on him or something—some mean thing to make him feel bad.

Mara always acts really weird around Jeremiah—even weirder than she does around the rest of us. They used to be friends, I think, but then she got mean. Now she's meaner to him than she is to anyone else.

I keep watching her, just in case. If she tries anything, I won't hesitate to step in. That's my jam. You don't mess with my friends. You don't want to see me go Doctor Robotnik on you, trust me.

But as Jeremiah hustles across the playground, Mara just watches him go. She doesn't throw rotten fruit or call out names or run up and stick a "kick me" note on his back or anything.

Weird. So much weird.

I'm itching to write it all down in my notebook. Mara would make the perfect villainess. And Jeremiah is the perfect shifty "What is he up to?" character.

I sit down and pull out my notebook and fill it with a thrilling and dastardly plot. My story is so hot, I'm surprised it doesn't burn up the page. This mouse video game is going to completely rock the world.

Finally, I drop my pen and look down at my watch. Zoinks! It's only a couple of minutes until the bell. I don't have time to go to the library. Being a super-observant game designer always on the lookout for gameplay ideas sure is distracting.

At the lockers, I run into Tom, who's getting his stuff out. He has some old-timey movie pictures taped inside his locker. I wish he'd tell me about those one day. He's clearly obsessed with them. There's gotta be some way I can incorporate old Hollywood into my games. He asks me about the mice, so I tell him all about my game idea as we walk to class.

Jeremiah's already in the hall outside the classroom, and he *still* looks all stressed out. I sidle over to him to see if he's okay.

"Dude. You good?"

Jeremiah nods and smiles. "Yeah. Just thinking."

"What about? The birds and the trees and stuff?"

"Always," he says, and his grin widens. "And mice now."

"So," I say, "you're vegetarian, right?"

"Vegan," he says. "I don't feel good about eating animals or wearing them. Animals are my friends, you know?"

"I'm thinking of having a vegan character in my new game," I tell him. "He'll help out the mice."

"You're making a game about the mice?" He nods. "I like the vibe of that."

I like the vibe of Jeremiah.

That's what I'm thinking as we go into class. He's a really good friend.

That's why what happens next is so darn weird.

Chapter 5

Yolanda, Tuesday, March 4, 8:42 a.m.

I watch Tom take his seat after making his accusation. He looks really happy to not be at the front of the class anymore.

Unlike Tom, I'm not nervous to speak to a group. When I'm a famous game designer, I'm totally going to be invited to talk at game cons *all* the time, so I need to get used to stuff like this. But . . . I kinda wish I was doing it for a different reason today.

"So, what do you think happened?" Jeremiah asks. He looks

curious and a bit confused, like a newborn puppy, except with hair braids. I feel bad about what I'm about to do.

I mean, I could just zip my lips, right? I could just say nothing. I could do a big dance routine to distract them . . .

If what I suspect is right, then Jeremiah did what he did with the best of intentions. Nobody will blame him for standing up for his beliefs. (Except maybe Mara—but she gets snarky if people breathe too loudly so, like, whatever, Mara.) If I don't say anything, then the mice might be gone for good. What if Jeremiah let them out over the back fence of the school? Everyone knows that stray cats hang out over that fence. Some kid once threw his chicken nuggets over there. (Which—*hello*? Why would you do that? *Chicken nuggets*!) There have been cats ever since. Everyone knows that the cats would eat the mice.

Except maybe for Jeremiah, who believes all animals are good and maybe even thinks that the stray cats would befriend the mice and invite them into their homes and offer them milk and cookies. Or cheese. Or bugs. Whatever. Stray cat afternoon tea.

I have to do this. I have to rat (or mouse?) on Jeremiah, even though he's my friend. It will be okay. Everyone likes Jeremiah. Nobody will be mad at him, will they?

I look again at Jeremiah's bemused, slightly weirded-out face. And I wish so much that it *had* been Mara who did it, so I didn't

have to do this. How is it that she always spoils everything, even when she's done nothing wrong?

I remind myself of the mice. And the cats, who have now morphed in my mind into old-timey bad guys, with fedora hats and cigars and gold-plated teeth. One of them is called "Catnip McGee."

To pump myself up for my accusation, I pretend I am at a game con. I pretend I have a little mic on my cheek and a loving audience in front of me. An audience full of my favorite game designers . . .

No, that just makes me totally nervous. My favorite game *characters* then. Yes!

Tom becomes Guybrush Threepwood from *Monkey Island*. Tom's sweet and funny, and he gets excited about stuff, like his movies, and he has blond hair, just like Guybrush.

Jeremiah is Gordon Freeman from *Half-Life.* He's kind of nerdy but also completely cool.

Jedda is Misty from *Pokémon*. She's way quieter than Misty, obviously, but just as kind.

And Mara? Well, Mara is Groose—the red-headed meanie from *Zelda*. I try to avoid looking at her.

I close my eyes. It helps. But, to be honest, not enough. The only thing I can think of that would make this a fun experience is . . .

I open my eyes and say it, as quickly as I can: "Our hero is the dashing young basketball player and talented student of architecture, Jeremiah Martin."

Everyone looks at me like I've suddenly turned blue and grown another nose.

"Hear me out, dudes, please," I say. "I'm nervous. Can I just do it this way? Like it's a game? That's what I do."

"Sure," Guybrush Threepwood—sorry, *Tom*—says slowly, "but what has that got to do with Jeremiah?"

"I mean . . ." I wince a little. "What if my game was called *Jeremiah's Great Lab Mouse-napping*?"

Jeremiah's mouth drops open, and my heart jolts a little, like I'm Sonic and I've just collided with a bunch of spikes.

Tom's eyes go all wide and intense, and he leans over his desk toward me. "*Lab Mice Heist!*"

"What?" I ask, thrown off track.

"That's the name of the movie!" Tom says.

"*What?*"

Jeremiah cuts in. "Guys, focus! Yolanda, you think I'm the one who took the mice?"

I turn back to him. "But I don't think you did it because you're a bad guy!" I blurt. "You're Gordon Freeman!"

"I'm . . . what?"

Everyone is looking at me with wide eyes. *Disbelieving* eyes.

Zoinks.

I shake my head. "I think you're totally awesome and funny and smart and kind and different in the best kind of way. I think you did it *because* you're kind and because you love animals and you don't think they should be kept in cages. I think you did it because you wanted them to be happy!"

Tom looks like he wants to say something, but I keep going before he can interrupt.

"And before everyone asks, I don't only think you did it because you're a kind-hearted vegan. I have more evidence! Here's how I think it happened." I scrunch my eyes closed and continue my video-game voiceover. "Jeremiah gets to school early—unusual for our hero. Usually, he's listening to some sick beats and talking to the birds and generally just being the sweet-hearted dreamer that he is. But this day—on the day of the *Lab Mice Heist*—he arrives early to sneak in and set the mice free . . ."

I think of the stray cats and their leader, Catnip McGee, who may, at this very moment, be settling in for an early brunch.

"Little does our hero know that there are bad cats over the fence—with cigars and everything! Well, they probably don't have cigars, but they *do* eat mice." I return to my normal voice. "And then, in a little box, we see an in-game movie of the cats, totally eating mice off little gold dinner plates."

"Ew!" the class responds.

I open one eye. They look enthralled by my game story. Which . . . feels good, if I'm being honest.

"Now we see Jeremiah doing the wicked deed—except it's not wicked, obviously, because he has such a good heart. We see him ducking through the open lobby doors, leaping over, like, laser beams and stuff that crisscross the hall! We see him dropping and rolling, so the janitor won't see him, somersaulting into our classroom, collecting the mice—*and ten Mice Heist points*—and racing back out of the classroom and running . . ."

I catch my breath. "Where, dude? Where do you run to? Where do you take the mice? Because, you know, you gotta tell us. Because we need to get the mice back! I mean, you saw the cats! In the in-game movie! Those suckers are *ruthless mouse murderers, dude*!"

I pause, finally.

I can't hear anything but stony silence. It's like when I'm in the middle of a game and the sound mutes and it takes me a second to work out what's going on, and then I realize that Mamá is next to me, holding the TV remote, and she's turned the sound off because it's time for dinner.

Everyone is staring at Jeremiah.

Jeremiah is staring at me.

"Dude?" My voice comes out like the croak of a bullfrog.

"It's because of my therapist," he says slowly.

"Your . . . what?"

"My therapist says I need to get to school earlier, so I won't feel so rushed. She thinks that will help me be calmer and settle more easily into the day."

"But you seemed so upset," I say. I feel my forehead wrinkling. "Or . . . distracted. Stressed. Not calm at all. And you *are* a vegan . . ."

"Yeah." Jeremiah grins. "A vegan, Yolanda. Not an idiot. I know there are stray cats over the fence, and I know they eat mice. There are plenty of other predators out there too. I might not like the mice being in a cage, but I know they're safer there than let loose on the school playground. I didn't let the mice out, Yolanda."

"Yes! All the Pop-Tarts!"

I turn around to see Tom pumping the air.

"What?" he asks. "Jeremiah's awesome. I don't want him to be the bad guy."

I glance past Tom to see that Mara's looking kinda pale, like a flour tortilla. Maybe because the heat's back on her? I see her mouth something that looks a lot like "Safer in the cage?"

But it could just as easily have been "Paper's all the rage." She's always on a hunt for the new cool thing. I wouldn't put it past her to have just discovered that paper is the new denim or whatever. Anyway, I don't care about Mara's trend obsessions right now (although, I am *so* not wearing paper jeans). I turn my attention back to Jeremiah.

"Really?" I feel like I've just gotten a one-up. And then the guilt takes over. "I'm so sorr—"

"Don't be," he interrupts. "If I were you, I might have thought the same thing. You didn't accuse me in a mean way. And I appreciate you noticing I looked upset. That's something only a good friend would do. Your game idea was *awesome*, by the way."

I feel my eyebrows shoot up. "You're not mad at me?"

"You should be!" Mara cries, throwing her hands up in the air. "It's not okay that she accused you!"

Jeremiah looks over at her calmly. "I knew it wasn't true, and I could prove it. And I know Yolanda didn't mean anything by it."

Mara rolls her eyes and huffs. She pulls out her body spray and gives it a half-hearted spritz. She seems comforted by the smell. It's blueberry today. It makes me feel, suddenly, super hungry for pie . . . I shake myself and tune back in to Jeremiah.

"Some of the bits she said were right, actually," he was saying. "Like the fact that I was stressed out . . . That actually has something to do with the mice. It has something to do with what *I* think happened to them."

"You have a theory too?" Tom asks.

Jeremiah nods. "Not just a theory, but the truth of what happened to the laboratory mice. Would you like to hear it?"

"Is *Castle of Illusion Starring Mickey Mouse* one of the most underrated Sega Genesis games of all time?" I ask.

"I don't know what that means," Jeremiah says, blinking at me.

"It means *obviously*, my friend." I take my seat and look at Jeremiah expectantly.

I'm looking forward to this. It's so much better listening to an accusation than making one. I almost wish I had popcorn.

Unless . . . He's not going to accuse me, is he?

Is he?

Chapter 6

Jeremiah, Tuesday, March 4, 8:20 a.m.

I am leaving early for school, and I'm feeling mildly stressed.

And the funny thing about it . . .

Or maybe it's not funny. It doesn't actually feel funny. The *peculiar* thing about it is that the reason I am leaving for school so early is to help me feel *less* stressed.

It's all Dr. Lim's idea. Or fault. Or both.

Dr. Lim is my therapist. Mostly, I like her a lot. She dresses in vibrant colors, which I like, and she likes Bruno Mars. Major points for that. Also, she works in a beautiful building, which I'm pretty sure was designed by the architect Paul Williams or, at the very least, is in his style. Paul Williams was the first African American member of the American Institute of Architects. He's my hero. That might sound boring. But I want to be an architect. Paul Williams is *everything* to me.

I'm getting distracted. I do that sometimes when I'm thinking about something that's really important to me.

I'm meant to be talking about Dr. Lim and her ideas. Or, specifically, this idea she has that being late makes me anxious. Which . . . is true. It makes sense that leaving for school earlier and walking there more quickly would make me feel calmer. But the truth is that it just means I have something else to worry about. Instead of worrying about leaving at 8:25 a.m., I have to worry about leaving at 8:20 a.m. And I don't get to do as much talking to the birds as I walk.

My dad meets me at the door with my messenger bag and headphones. "Forgetting something?" he asks. He gives me that raised-eyebrows look he does that makes him look almost exactly like Dr. Cockroach from *Monsters, Inc.*

He squeezes my shoulder and says, "This will get easier. You'll get used to leaving earlier, and you'll feel calmer because of it, and everything will get better."

My dad says that all the time: "Everything will get better." It's like his catchphrase, along with "I will help you fix this" and "You are not alone" and "Why is there no root beer left, Jeremiah?"

My dad is a pro at making me feel better (apart from when he does the root beer thing. Those times, I run to my room and hide the root beer bottles).

Bruno Mars helps too. I plug my headphones into my phone. We're not allowed phones at school, but it's okay to have them before school. Mine pretty much only makes calls and plays music, which is fine because I don't use the internet that much, except to download music and read architecture websites.

I hug my dad, put on my headphones, and set off.

I try to keep my eyes focused forward as I walk, to stop me from getting distracted by birds and such. I do spot a particularly interesting little sparrow bobbing along a wall, and I can't resist stopping to say hi to him, but I only do it quickly.

In my ears, Bruno is singing "Talking to the Moon," which is one of my favorite songs, because sometimes I talk to the moon too. I really hope Mara never finds out about that habit. As soon as she finds out anything about me, she talks about it all the time.

Mara and I used to be friends when we first started elementary school. She was really, really quiet—she hardly ever said anything. She used to have all these appointments after school. (I don't know what they were for—we were really little, so I never thought to ask,

although I figured they were for some secret superhero business because that's what always happened in my books.) She didn't really have any other friends, but we played together during recess.

Even then, Mara and I didn't have much in common—I liked music and building stuff with blocks, and she liked perfume and fashion and looking stuff up on the computer. But it was okay. We were little, so it didn't really matter. (Back then, she'd let me have a squirt of her body sprays sometimes, which was bizarrely cool to me. I loved that chocolate one *so much*.)

But then, one summer vacation, Mara went away for a while. When she came back, she talked a lot. Some of the other kids started getting mad at her because she said mean things about them. She started arguing a lot with Yolanda and Tom. Because I was friends with them and it did seem like Mara was being the mean one, I stopped being friends with her. It felt bad, but it was just kind of easier that way.

Since then, it seems like she cannot stop saying mean things. Sometimes, the mean things are about me.

I don't like it when people make fun of me. I especially don't like it when Mara does, because we used to be friends. So I don't want her to know about the moon chats.

I'm almost to the school gates when I get properly distracted. But it's for a good reason! A little dog—maybe a Yorkshire terrier or a cairn terrier (it is hard to tell, because the dog is moving at a remarkable speed)—races by. It is trailing a long pink leather leash. I take off my headphones and turn around, trying to figure out what's going on.

I can hear its owner calling out, "Nutter Butter! Nutter Butter, get back here!"

For a second, I almost don't chase the dog. It just looks so happy and free, running away from its owner, its leash trailing behind it like a rainbow shooting out of a unicorn . . .

But I know that Nutter Butter's owner will be sad if he is lost for good. So I do the right thing. I take a big leap—which I'm good at because I play basketball—and jump right on top of Nutter Butter's leash.

Nutter Butter stops quickly and falls on his back. He jumps back up and turns to look at me with a really dirty look on his face.

Sorry, Nutter Butter. It was for your own good.

His owner thanks me a bunch of times and shakes my hand and calls me "young fellow" and tries to give me some money, but I say no to that, because you don't do good things for money, do you?

Catching the dog makes me think of the mice in our classroom. That dog looked so happy to be free. I am sure that the mice wish to be free, too—especially free from that horrible, poorly designed plastic cage. If it was up to me, those mice would be in an architecturally designed *castle*.

One of Dr. Lim's other suggestions was that, when I get to school early, I should sit under a tree for a few minutes to meditate. I've never been good at meditating in her office, but she thinks that being in nature might do the trick.

My favorite tree in the school playground is a very old valley oak at the edge of the sports field. I'm just heading over to it when I hear her voice.

Ms. Abaza. I'd know her voice anywhere. But she doesn't sound peaceful and happy, like she usually does. She sounds really, really upset! I might not always be good at working out how people are feeling or what they mean, but I can definitely tell when someone is super distressed, and that's exactly how Ms. Abaza sounds right now.

She sounds like how I would sound if someone took away my headphones. Or if I had just read that there would be no more music, or . . . Maybe if a giant bear was running after me?

Okay, maybe not that bad.

"I can't believe I did that! It's just . . . so not *like* me. Oh rats!" she says. She's standing where the playground meets the parking lot.

I hear another teacher call out her name. Ms. Abaza gives a little shriek and drops all of her folders. She bends down to pick them up. The other teacher—Mr. Paine, the gym teacher—helps her tidy them up, apologizing for startling her.

"I am so on edge today," she tells him. "Something really *awful* has happened! I just . . . I spent so much *money* and now . . . poof! Gone! Just like that. I'm so stupid. It was all my fault."

She straightens and looks at Mr. Paine intently. "Actually, John, maybe you can help me with my problem. You can help me find . . ."

Mr. Paine hands her the folders. They start walking together toward the school, so I can't hear any more of what they say, but I'm super curious.

I really like Ms. Abaza. She's always extra kind to me and always helps me out when I'm feeling stressed. I hope the awful thing that's happened to her isn't too awful!

I remember she once told me that she left a bag on the bus with some Bruno Mars CDs in it (she is old, so she still listens to CDs)—and she *never got them back.*

I hope it's not something as awful as that. Ms. Abaza might be clumsy and scatterbrained sometimes, but nobody deserves to lose her music.

Then I get to thinking . . .

My dad's a lawyer. Sometimes, he tells me about his cases and the criminals he has to prosecute. Some of those criminals are robbers and thieves.

What if Ms. Abaza had something stolen from her?! She did say she had spent a lot of money . . .

I have to stop my brain a bit. Sometimes, I get carried away with thoughts, and I mix things up. I'm sure that's why I'm mixing up my dad's work and Ms. Abaza. I'm sure there's a simple explanation for everything.

I finally make it to the oak tree.

It's the one Jedda sometimes climbs, but she's not here now. I put my headphones on the ground because Dr. Lim says it's best to either have music with no lyrics or just silence when you're meditating, because the words can be a distraction.

Bruno Mars's words are especially distracting to me because . . . I mean, it's *Bruno Mars*, man. I have no instrumental music on my phone, so silence it is.

Except, of course, our school playground is not silent at all. Kids are fitting in a final few minutes of freedom before school starts. It's loud and boisterous and squealing and thumping, and I can't concentrate at all.

I try and distract myself from the noise by thinking of a single word. Dr. Lim says that picking a word and repeating it over and over in your head can help block out other "stimuli"—stuff that interests or excites your brain. She suggested I use "om" or "ham-sah."

Today, I use the word "mouse."

I string it out as long as I can and say it in a really low voice and pretend I'm a Buddhist monk.

Unfortunately, the more I do my mouse chant, the more I think about the actual mice in their non-architecturally designed cage, and the more distracted I get from my meditation. I try switching the word to "ho'oponopono," which is a Hawaiian mantra word Dr. Lim suggested. She was born in Hawai'i (just like Bruno Mars!). The mantra word has to do with gratitude and forgiveness.

Using that word actually does make me feel a bit better. It makes me think about all the things I have to be grateful about, and it reminds me that I should try and be forgiving of people. Even when they are mean to me, like Mara is.

An alarm on my phone goes off. I realize I'll have to really *hustle*—which is a word I learned from Yolanda—to make it to my class's Before-School Hall Party in time.

Luckily, I hustle so fast I'm one of the first people there. It helps that Dad got my books organized before school, so I don't have to stop at my locker. Yolanda comes along not long after. We chat for a minute or two about game design and veganism and stuff.

I realize I actually am feeling okay. Definitely not as stressed as I usually feel at the start of the day. Maybe there's something to be said for this meditation thing and for being organized.

Or maybe there's just something to be said for chatting with a friend.

I'm feeling good when we walk into class.

But then, of course, everything gets peculiar.

Chapter 7

Jeremiah, Tuesday, March 4, 8:45 a.m.

Maybe I should be mad at Yolanda for accusing me of letting the mice out, but I'm not.

She says that she only thought I was the culprit because I am a good person who cares about animal rights. This is true. It's also true that I was thinking a lot about the mice wishing to be free. Maybe if I were a different kind of person—the sort of person who acts impulsively and doesn't worry about consequences—I would have let them out. But I'm not that sort of person. I know that letting the mice go free would be wrong for many reasons:

1.) It would be very distressing for Ms. Abaza, who I really like. She would probably blame herself and feel guilty. I don't want that, especially as she's having a bad day already.
2.) It would be disappointing for my classmates and friends, because they are excited about studying the mice.
3.) There are big stray cats lurking outside the school. There are also predatory birds. It would be a mouse apocalypse.

So I didn't do it. But I'm a bit worried about admitting who I think the culprit was. Especially because my theory might just be my thoughts running away from me . . .

But I gotta do this. Because Mouse Apocalypse.

"I think it was an international crime organization," I say.

Even though I don't say it in a dramatic, sort of "Hollywood movie" way like Tom did, the whole class gasps. I can't blame them. It sounds like something straight out of a movie or a video game. Tom and Yolanda are staring at me with matching wide-eyed expressions.

"Wait!" I tell my classmates as they start whispering to each other. "Just . . . let me explain."

The whispers shush, and my classmates turn back to look at me.

"Just tell us what you mean, dude," Yolanda says gently. She must know that it's a bit hard for me to talk to the whole class like this.

Tom adds, "We're listening, Jeremiah. Don't be nervous. Just tell us what you're thinking."

He gets up from his seat and sits on an empty desk a bit closer to where I'm standing at the front. Yolanda does the same, and so does Jedda. Some of the other kids also come closer. They do it in a friendly way—almost like they want to show me that they're with me.

There's no way I can avoid it. I have to tell my classmates about my theory.

"I heard Ms. Abaza talking to Mr. Paine—he was helping her pick up some folders she'd dropped—and she said that something really bad had happened and she needed his help looking for something. I wonder if she was talking about the mice. I wonder if she already knew that the mice were stolen and she was feeling bad about it."

"So you think there are real criminals involved?" asks Yolanda. To herself, she whispers something that sounds a lot like "*Katniss McPhee.*"

"I mean, maybe? She also said she had spent a bunch of

money, so . . . What if the mice are really valuable mice? Like, some kind of rare breed? I don't know much about fancy mice, but I know that some pets can cost millions of dollars, like Tibetan mastiffs and stuff. There are even people who buy stag beetles for, like, a hundred grand or something. So it's possible they were expensive mice. Or maybe they just belonged to some mobster's daughter?" I lean against Ms. Abaza's desk. I'm feeling a bit light-headed from all the talking.

"*Catnip McPhee* . . . ," Yolanda whispers. She's in a weird mood today. Maybe she stayed up too late playing computer games. I've never done that, because I don't really play video games, but I stayed up late listening to music once and woke up with pizza stuck to my face.

Jedda clears her throat. Everyone looks at her. Jedda doesn't talk much at all, so every time she does, we can't help but look.

"I don't know, Jeremiah," she says. "I mean, it sounds like it could be *possible*, but without any hard evidence—"

"There's more," I say. "Ms. Abaza's late to class. Maybe she's out there, talking to the police about the million-dollar missing mice? That's more evidence, isn't it?"

"Yeah . . . ," Jedda says slowly.

"But it seems . . . unlikely?" Tom says this kindly. "I watch enough movies—I mean, I know it's *possible*, but isn't it more likely that Ms. Abaza just made a mistake with the mice? She can be a bit clumsy."

He's right. Before school, I saw her drop a bunch of folders. And yesterday . . .

"Yesterday, I noticed she didn't close the cage lid properly, so I fixed it," I say. "She *is* clumsy. So it's Ms. Abaza's fault? And not the gangsters?"

This thought makes my chest hurt. It sounds like I am accusing our teacher—who we love—of doing something that would upset many of us. Ms. Abaza would never intentionally try to upset us. She's the sort of teacher who lets Yolanda go on the computers for extra time, because she knows how much Yolanda loves it. She lets Tom leave early to go to soccer practice. She once let me build a pillow fort in the corner when everything was getting too loud and too bright and too out of control. And she hardly ever growls at Mara, even when Mara might deserve it. (Like when she's spraying that body spray she loves so much.) Ms. Abaza would be heartbroken if she lost the mice we were so excited about.

"Zoinks," says Yolanda.

I push myself backward, so I'm sitting on Ms. Abaza's desk. Usually, that's not allowed, but she's not here right now, and I figure, given what's going on, she probably wouldn't mind so much if she did walk in.

"But if you fixed the cage, how did the mice get free?" Tom asks.

Jedda bites her lip. "And if Ms. Abaza was involved, do you think she would get in trouble? I mean, there must be rules about making sure that you don't lose track of school property. I reckon the janitor would be annoyed, too, and probably the canteen—I mean *cafeteria* lady? About having mice running around?"

She leans back on her desk. "Once, I accidentally let my pet skink, Irwin, free in the house, and he ate all the fruit off the pavlova that Mum made for a party. She was so annoyed. I wasn't allowed to watch *Saddle Club* for a whole week. I don't want Ms. Abaza to get punished like that. That was *brutal*. Not that I think she watches *Saddle Club*. But maybe, like, the National Geographic Channel or whatever it is teachers watch in their spare time?"

Jedda finally takes a breath, and we all stare at her. I've never heard her talk so much!

She actually looks a bit nervous . . .

"We're all worried about that, Jedda," Tom says softly. "About making false accusations. In fact, I don't think there's anyone in this class who we really do want to blame." His eyes flick over to Mara, and he looks a bit guilty. "But we have to, or the mice might die. And Jeremiah's theory is probably the most probable of any of the ones we've had. Not the gangster part. The gangster part was—sorry, Jeremiah—bananas."

"If I was playing a game," Yolanda says, "and I came across a character who made me answer a multiple-choice question before I could get to the treasure or whatever, and the question was 'Who out of these people is most likely to have let the mice out?' I think I'd be going with Ms. Abaza right now. Even though I wasn't the one who thought of her."

"So, unless you have any other ideas . . . ," Tom begins.

"Well," says Jedda, "that's the thing. I kind of do."

I have a warm feeling in my belly when she says this. I feel kind of happy and floating. I guess I'm relieved. I never wanted it to be Ms. Abaza or an international crime boss. I never wanted it to be me either. But the thing is—like Tom says—I don't really want it to be anyone in our class. Not even Mara—who's holding her body spray right now like it's a teddy bear. She looks kind of . . . sad and lost. It makes me feel icky. Maybe she's not as bad as I thought she was.

"Who is it?" asks Yolanda. "Who do you think let the mice out?"

Jedda looks around the classroom in silence for a minute. Each time she meets someone's eyes, that person looks as scared and self-conscious as Mara.

But then, finally, Jedda says something that makes my heart soar.

"The thing is," she says, "I don't think *anyone* let the mice out. I think . . . they let *themselves* out. It all started yesterday afternoon . . ."

Chapter 8

Jedda, Monday,
March 3, 3:00 p.m.

It's my least favorite part of the day (apart from before school and lunchtime and recess, of course). Everyone is packing up around me. My heart is beating so heavily that I can hear it echoing around the room. I don't want to be too stereotypically Aussie, but it really feels like I have a big, fat wombat stomping around in my chest.

Soon, I'm going to have to get up too. But . . . what if I do it too early? What if I run into someone in the corridor? And I have to *talk* to them?

I know, I'm making it sound like they're all scary monsters who might bite me if I met them out there—and they're not. They're all totally nice, normal, non-monstery kids—but you have to believe me when I tell you that it's a big deal for me.

I remember when I was a little girl. I'd go with my family to the beach, down at Nubeena. We'd cook yabbies (a kind of funky little blue crayfish) on an open fire, sing songs, and tell stories. Jarrah and I would find big shells and hold them up to our ears. Jarrah said it sounded like the ocean to him. To me, it sounded like the ocean's heartbeat.

I can hear it now, in my ears. The ocean's heartbeat. Except it's *my* heartbeat, really. And it's not because of a shell. It's because I feel nervous.

I hate the end of the day at Checkerbloom Elementary. Back in Tassie (which is what we call Tasmania—we shorten pretty much everything in Australia, just ask the roos and the crocs!), the end of school was the best bit of the day. I'd race out of class with my mates. We'd go and find Jarrah and his mates, and we'd all walk together to the milk bar for an ice cream or some hot chips and sauce (hot chips are what we call french fries, by the way). Then we'd all go to one of our houses and do our homework together, and then we'd run outside again, to hang out and skate and climb trees and play netball and stuff, 'til it started to get dark and our mums came out of the houses and called out our names.

The end of the school day in Tassie was great.

Here, it's just scary. Because here, I have no mates. Here, the kids aren't like me. Or, I guess, I'm not like them. They don't talk the way I do, and they don't know any of the places I know. They don't even know what *Saddle Club* is (it's my favorite TV show back home).

I feel like an alien.

I feel so far from home. A world away from my beach. My ocean. There is plenty of ocean here, of course. But it's not the same. It's not *mine*. And I guess that's part of why the end of the day is not so great here. Because I'm not going home.

The other, bigger part is because I'm scared of the hallways. I just want to get out of the school without anyone seeing me. Without anyone asking me, for the hundredth time, "Is it true you have kangaroos bouncing down the street where you come from?" (The answer, by the way, is no. We do have wallabies bouncing down the street, though, and they're pretty much just mini kangaroos, but with added fluff and cuteness.)

So, what I tend to do is stay behind, while Ms. Abaza and the other kids go out. I pretend I'm just packing up my things *really* slowly. But once I've done that, I open my notebook, and

I do some sketching. I love to sketch. It makes me feel a lot less anxious. I usually find a Tim Tam or two to eat while I'm doing it.

Today, while my classmates file out, I start off drawing pictures of the mice, because they're what's in my head.

I give them my own names. I thought of them during class, while the other kids were arguing about their ideas. I didn't say mine out loud, though, obviously. They're all in my people's language—Palawa kani. They are:

- Lutana, which means "moon," because there's one that's pure white, like the moon;
- Rayakana, which means "song," because one of them never stopped squeaking, and its squeaks sounded a bit like singing;
- Redpa, which means "mosquito," because one kept biting the others;
- Rrala, which means "strong," because one of them is really little, but still seemed to be fighting hard for her place in the family; and
- Timita, which means "possum," because one had a little curly tail that reminded me of a ringtail possum tail.

I'll never tell my classmates the names I chose for the mice, of course. They'd make fun of me and tell me the names sound

dumb. But I liked coming up with them, and I like drawing the mice.

I draw the mice climbing up a mountain. I give them teeny little climbing poles and beanies with pom-poms on top, and I draw one barfing, because Jarrah always barfs on bushwalks. He blames the altitude. I blame the massive bag of Cheezels he eats while we're walking.

I finish my drawing with some woolly butt gum trees—the kind you see on the mountain near my home. It makes me a bit sad, drawing those. I miss them.

Finally, when I think the coast is completely clear, I shove my notebook into my bag and sling my bag over my shoulder. Then I walk toward the door.

But something stops me just as I walk outside the classroom. Maybe it's the noise of one of the mice squeaking. Maybe it's something else. Whatever it is, it makes me turn. I look back into the classroom.

That's when I see it—a faint glow, coming from the cage on Ms. Abaza's desk! And I see one of the mice sort of . . . *illuminated*.

Like the *mouse* is *glowing*.

My heart speeds up.

I really love science, especially physics and chemistry, and my favorite scientist is Marie Curie. She was one of the first scientist

to study radioactivity. She discovered two radioactive chemicals: polonium and radium. *Both of which glow.*

And both can make you very sick or even kill you!

Ms. Abaza is also known for her love of science . . .

On my first day of school, when I told her I loved Marie Curie, she told me about her grandfather's watch. It was made back in the time when painting watch faces with radium was really popular, because it made the numbers glow in the dark. That would have been like having smartphone watches now, I reckon. Like, people would have thought it was amazing.

I didn't ask Ms. Abaza if she still had her grandfather's watch. I don't even know if a radium-painted watch would still glow after all these years, but what if . . .

What if she does still have it at home? What if she didn't realize it would still be dangerous after all this time? What if she kept the mice at her house before she brought them in here, and they are now radioactive? *What if they mutate?*

This is not good. I have to tell someone.

I run into the hall, toward the principal's office, my heart now an Australian tiger beetle (which is, by the way, the fastest insect on Earth).

I'm halfway down the hallway when it hits me—the strong, sweet, unmistakable smell of bubble gum body spray. Then she turns the corner . . .

It's Mara, and she's heading back toward our classroom!

"Don't go in there!" I call out, screeching to a stop in front of her. "It's full of radioactive mice!"

"I'm not going in there!" Mara says quickly.

She sounds a bit jumpy, and she's hiding something behind her back. I only get a quick glimpse of it, but I see it's bottle-shaped and wrapped in pink tissue paper.

"Wait, what?" she adds, as if she's only just realized what I said. "*Radioactive* mice?"

I hold my breath, expecting her to scream.

Instead, Mara rolls her eyes and laughs. "You think the mice are radioactive? You're so weird. You're imagining things."

"I'm not!" I protest. I can feel my cheeks burning. I've never talked to Mara, really, and she has a reputation for being a bit mean. But I have to argue with her now. I can't let anyone be in danger. "I saw them glowing."

"You are so weird," Mara says. "Mice don't glow. I bet it's just some glow-in-the-dark stickers that Ms. Abaza brought in to show us. Trust me, if you tell anyone to come to the classroom to check it out, they're just going to laugh at you. You don't want that, do you? People already think you're weird, because of your accent and stuff—'G'day, mate!'"

I try so hard to stifle an eye-roll it hurts my head.

It's true, though. I don't want to be laughed at. I don't want to draw any attention to myself at all. I shake my head. "No."

Mara smiles tightly. "Good. Now, just . . . run along home. I mean, I know you don't have an *actual* home here, but . . . you know what I mean."

My cheeks are on fire. I turn around without saying another word and leave Mara in the hallway.

And I realize she's right. I must have just imagined the glow. Or maybe it is stickers. Whatever the case, I probably shouldn't tell anyone. I don't want anyone to think I'm more of a freak than they already do.

I'm relieved, of course. I mean, who wants radioactive mice? Radioactive *mutant* mice? I know the turtles were cool but, seriously, only in cartoon form. Real-life mutant mice would not be so much fun, even if they brought pizza with them. (Actually, pizza-delivering mutant mice might not be such a bad idea . . .)

I'm hungry. That's what it is! It's messing with my brain. I need to get home, right away, and eat something. Probably pizza. With pineapple on top, because that's how we Australians roll.

I hope that Mara forgets everything I said about radioactive mice. Otherwise, tomorrow is going to be terrible.

Tuesday, March 4, 8:22 a.m.

I walk to school, thinking about mice and Marie Curie and home.

It's only been a couple of days since my cousin Merindah started letting me walk to school by myself. Before this, she walked me every day. While I appreciated it, I know it made her a bit late to work, and besides, she only lives five minutes away, and this is a really safe neighborhood (as everyone keeps telling me).

Plenty of the other kids walk to school too. I see Jeremiah walking by himself, listening to music, and Yolanda with one of her mothers. I see Tom walking with his sister.

I see Mara too. She's alone, like I am. She's walking on the opposite side of the road from Jeremiah, but she seems to be keeping pace. If I didn't know better, I'd say she was following him. Why would Mara follow Jeremiah?

Everyone at school says Mara is mean, and sometimes, it seems like she is. But sometimes, it seems like she's just a bit blunt, like Jarrah. He's always telling me when I need a shower or when my hair looks funny or that my joke about a lazy baby kangaroo being a "pouch potato" is really dumb. It's fine. I kind of like it, because I know he'll never let me make a fool of myself.

I could really do with some of his bluntness now. I can't stop thinking about the glowing mice. I stayed awake for hours last night thinking about it.

What if Mara was wrong?

What if there *are* Teenage Mutant Ninja Mice? What if they've run away and started fighting crime in the city? What if they didn't meet their "Splinter" and they've become bad guys? Because nobody gave them pizza and they got really *hangry*?

What if they start eating other animals or something? The kids in my class would never forgive me if that happened. Especially Jeremiah! He's a vegan!

What if I was wrong to just go home and not tell anyone? I mean, the pizza was good, but if the mice are mutants? I'm completely doomed. No pizza is worth that. Even Tim Tams wouldn't be worth that.

Chapter 9

Jedda, Tuesday, March 4, 8:51 a.m.

I tell the kids in Ms. Abaza's class about what I think happened to our laboratory mice.

I don't start out with Teenage Mutant Ninja Mice. I start out with *science*, which to me is even cooler.

"Radium was discovered by Marie and Pierre Curie in 1898," I tell them.

I expect their eyes to start glazing over or for the yawning and fidgeting to begin. But as I gaze around the room, I notice nobody actually seems bored. Everyone is listening to me, even Mara.

It gives me a bit of confidence. I don't perch up on Ms. Abaza's desk, like Jeremiah did. Instead, I start to pace at the front of the room, imagining myself as a university professor, lecturing in chemistry. That helps a bit with the nerves.

"At first, radium was used in self-luminous paints for watches, nuclear panels, aircraft switches, clocks, and instrument dials. I should have explained. . . . Radium becomes luminescent—that means that it glows—when it starts to decay."

"Like glow-in-the-dark stickers," Mara says darkly.

I try to ignore her.

And, I mean, she's wrong. Modern glow-in-the-dark stickers are mostly made from an alkaline earth metal called aluminate, with some other stuff, like europium or dysprosium, mixed in with it. I looked it up last night. Not so scary.

Not so mutant-making.

"Radium was used in heaps of stuff, back before people discovered that the effects of radium—or radiation—can cause cancer. There were a whole lot of women back then who worked in factories that made the glowing things. They got really sick and died. They were called the Radium Girls. And I read that—in addition to causing cancer—radium's ionizing radiation, like, blasts all the surrounding tissue with charged particles, which can destroy DNA and cause mutations. That's some *scary science*. And on my first day here, I told Ms. Abaza I loved Marie Curie, and she told me her grandfather had a radium watch!"

I take a deep breath, spreading my arms wide. "So that's my theory. I'm really worried Ms. Abaza has the watch now, and that she left the mice near the watch and they've gone . . . mutant."

The class begins to chatter and gasp in shock. I talk over them. "I mean, it's maybe not true, and I know Ms. Abaza knows a lot about science stuff, so it seems unlikely she wouldn't know everything about radium, but she does seem a bit scatterbrained sometimes, and—"

"Wait!" Yolanda interrupts me. "So you think there are *mutant mice* running around?" She pulls out her little notebook. "I am *so* stealing that for my game."

I nod. "When I left the classroom yesterday afternoon, the cage was *glowing*. And remember how Jeremiah said that Ms. Abaza was upset? What if she suddenly realized the radium might be harmful? What if she was looking for the mice with Mr. Paine? To stop them going rogue?"

My classmates exchange looks and start nodding. They believe me.

I gulp. If they believe me about the radium, then they will also believe that I knew about it yesterday and that there are possibly murderous mice out there.

Yolanda seems to read my mind. "Hang on, dude," she says, dropping her pen, her eyes widening. "So you're telling me there might be *actual* giant rodents out there in the streets? Wouldn't they be dangerous?"

"Oh my gosh!" Tom squeaks. "I've seen *Godzilla* five times. This is not going to end well."

"This is awful!" Jeremiah adds. "There are so many amazing buildings in this city—they'll be *crushed*!" His head drops to his hands.

My classmates begin to talk more loudly. Some of them get up from their seats to look out the windows. It's a disaster. And it's all my fault!

"Wait!" A voice rings out through the chaos.

I hear it, but nobody else seems to.

"Wait!" The voice yells again.

Then the strong scent of blueberries fills the room. Everyone stops now and turns in the direction of Mara.

She holds her body spray bottle in one hand, like it's an air horn or something. In her other hand, she holds a phone, which is not at all allowed at school, but Mara is just the sort of kid to ignore that rule.

"I googled it," she says calmly. "I looked up today's local news. No mutant mice. Everyone, take a chill pill."

I can't help it. I burst into tears.

"What's wrong?" Tom asks. "This is *good* news. No mutant mice!"

I shake my head. "Now you're going to think I'm crazy, like Mara said. You all already hate me!"

There's silence for a moment while everyone stares at me.

Finally, Tom says, "Jedda, nobody hates you. We're all really interested in you. We want to know about what it's like in Tasmania—like, are there really yetis there, and is it true that all the snakes are poisonous? We worry you don't like us because you don't talk much. But we think you seem really smart!"

"And you're definitely good at climbing trees," Jeremiah adds.

My cheeks burn. "No yetis. They're called bunyips." I don't tell them that bunyips aren't real either. Because . . . what if they are? Who knows?

"And . . ." I turn to Jeremiah. "You see me climbing the tree?"

Jeremiah smiles and shrugs. "I'm supposed to meditate under it," he says. "So I stare at it sometimes, trying to make myself go over to it and say 'om.' "

"We all like you," Yolanda chimes in. She stands up and moves to my side. "And nobody will blame you for not telling. It's totally understandable. We might"—She narrows her eyes as she looks around the classroom. Her eyes lock on to Mara's—"blame someone else though," she finishes. "When did Mara say you were crazy?"

I sniff. "Yesterday afternoon. She told me I shouldn't tell anyone that the cage was glowing and the mice were mutating—or not."

Mara inches toward the door.

"Hey!" Yolanda calls out. She walks until she's standing almost nose to nose with Mara. "Where do you think you're going? You stay here. Tell us why exactly you told Jedda not to tell anyone about what she saw."

Mara's leaf-green eyes widen. She takes a step away from Yolanda and holds up her hands. "I can explain," she says.

I walk away from the front of the classroom. I'm not the center of attention anymore, and it feels good.

It also feels good when Tom grabs my arm and guides me to stand by him. He gives me a little smile and waggles his eyebrows.

And I think . . . it might be nice to have a friend like Tom. And one like Yolanda. And one like Jeremiah. Maybe things won't be so bad here from now on.

Before I can think too much about the future, Mara clears her throat. She walks toward the front of the classroom and stands where I was only a moment before.

I sit beside Tom. Yolanda and Jeremiah take their seats too. With the rest of the class, we watch Mara, waiting to hear what she has to say.

"The thing is . . . ," she says, "it was almost definitely aliens."

Chapter 10

Tuesday, March 4, 9:00 a.m.

"Aliens!" Tom exclaimed. "Like a sci-fi movie. I *love* sci-fi movies. I give them more Pop-Tarts than any other genre! *Pop-Tarts for the aliens!*"

"Aliens. *Zoinks*," Yolanda whispered, imagining where she could add them to her game.

Jedda just looked at Mara, who was leaning on Ms. Abaza's desk and gripping her body spray tightly. Mara's hands were shaking. She looked really nervous. She cleared her throat and squeezed her eyes tightly shut.

Jedda and Jeremiah exchanged a look.

"Mara?" said Jedda finally. "What's wrong? It's going to be okay. Just talk."

Mara opened her eyes. They were shining with tears.

"I don't know why I am the way I am," she said quietly. "I don't mean to be. Everything I say j-just comes out the wrong way. I just want to be friends with you all, but it all goes so wrong, and I hurt everyone."

This was not what the others were expecting. They watched Mara in shocked silence.

"Mom always says that things will get better. She says that I should just be myself and people will like me. It hasn't happened yet . . ." Mara trailed off, staring into space. She gave her body spray bottle a sad little pump.

"Wait . . . ," said Yolanda slowly, when it was clear that Mara wasn't going to start talking again. "What does this have to do with aliens?"

Mara waved her spray bottle in the air. "I lied. That stuff never happens in real life. I know, because I google stuff all the time, so I know most things. I just—I don't want you to be mad."

"Mara?" Yolanda said.

"Yes?"

"Just tell us the truth." Yolanda smiled at Mara. "It's okay. I can see how anxious you are. Sometimes, my mom gets like that—all shaky and stuff. I know this must be hard for you, but you need to tell us the truth."

"We won't be mad," Tom added.

"We'll listen," Jedda said. She pulled her backpack onto her lap and rummaged around in it for a moment. Finally, she found a packet of chocolate cookies. She passed the packet over to Tom. "Take one and pass it on," she said. "These are Tim Tams. They make everything better. Trust me. Eat these while you listen to Mara's story." She nodded at Mara. "It'll all be okay, mate," she said.

"We definitely won't be mad—if you let me steal the aliens idea for my mouse computer game," Yolanda finished.

"All right," Mara said, sniffing. "I will. But you have to believe me."

"I think," Tom said slowly, "that at this point, we'll all believe almost anything." He nodded at Mara. "Go on. Tell us what really happened to the lab mice."

Mara took a deep, shaky breath, and then cried out through her tears, "You were right, Tom. I did set the mice free!"

"Zoinks! So you admit it!" Yolanda said. "You were the one who pulled off the lab mice heist yesterday afternoon!"

"I did," Mara muttered. "But I had a good reason. And I *didn't* do it yesterday afternoon."

"But then why were you heading to the classroom?" Jedda asked.

Mara bit her lip. "I went there to . . ." She turned her attention to Jeremiah. "Jeremiah, look inside your desk," she mumbled.

Jeremiah was really confused. "Why—"

"Just do it."

Jeremiah opened his desk lid slowly, expecting a mutant mouse to jump out. Instead, he saw a pink-paper-wrapped, bottle-shaped package.

"Open it," Mara said quietly.

Jeremiah did as he was told. Inside the package, there was a bottle of *boy's* chocolate body spray.

He looked up at Mara. "What is—"

"I bought it so you'd like me," she said. "I miss being friends with you, like we used to be. I remembered you said you liked the chocolate body spray, and I found the one for boys. But then, when I got home, I thought it wasn't *enough*. It wasn't enough to make you like me. Make you want to be my friend again."

She looked up and met his dark-brown eyes. "I know I say things that sound mean sometimes. The thing is . . . I used to stutter when I was really little, and it's much better now, but sometimes, I say things in a big b-blurt, before I think them through properly, and they come out all wrong, and I especially hate it when it happens with you. *You* thought it was mean to keep the mice in a cage. I wanted . . . I wanted to do what you wanted. I wanted to impress you."

Jeremiah looked even more stunned.

"Because I really like you," Mara added. She was crying again. "If you don't believe me, take a look at this."

She reached into her pocket and pulled out a folded piece of paper. She took it over to Jeremiah and put it in his hand. Jeremiah unfolded the paper and read. Everyone watched him in silence.

When he was done, Jeremiah refolded the piece of paper and gave it back to Mara.

"Well?" said Yolanda. "What does it say?'

"Can I tell?" Jeremiah asked.

Mara nodded, blushing.

"It's the names of some Bruno Mars songs," he said to Yolanda. He looked back at Mara curiously.

"I know you like him," she said. "I was going to google some of his songs so I could talk to you about them. Then, if I did that, I thought you might be my friend."

She let out a big, gulping sob. "But it's not just Jeremiah! I really want to be friends with all of you, but I always seem to mess it up! The thing is, I really like all of you, and as soon as I got to class, I realized I was wrong to have let the mice out. I realized how mad and upset you all were. I promise I didn't mean to upset any of you. I just wanted you to like me."

There was a long, long pause after Mara finished talking. She was sure that the classroom walls were closing in on her.

Finally, it was Jedda who spoke. "So, I'm new here," she said. "But where I come from, at my old primary school—that's what we call elementary school in Tasmania—we were taught that you should never hold grudges and that you should always forgive. I forgive you, Mara. I think you were trying to be a good friend. You went about it the wrong way, but I went about getting friends the wrong way too. You don't find friends when you're hiding up a tree. Unless you want to be friends with birds."

"Nothing wrong with that," said Jeremiah.

Jedda smiled. "I forgive you, Mara, and I hope everyone else does too."

"I forgive you," Jeremiah said quickly.

Yolanda rolled her eyes. "Me, too, I guess."

"And me," said Tom.

Mara felt a weight lift from her shoulders.

Tom added, "As long as you stop teasing me about the pictures in my locker or calling me 'Starlet.' " He looked around at his classmates. He seemed to be thinking something over. Finally, he took a deep breath. "I like old movie stars. And movies. *A lot*."

Yolanda shrugged. "I like old video games. Everyone has their thing."

"I promise I won't tease you anymore," Mara said. "I'm sorry I said that dumb stuff."

"Okay." Yolanda hopped up off her seat. "Let's just agree that Mara is sorry and we forgive her. But we really had better go and find those mice before Catnip McGee eats their little tails off. Now, Mara, how did you get the mice out of here without the cage? And where did you take them?"

Mara's face darkened. She held up her glittery handbag. "I carried them in here," she said, "and they *peed* in it, and it *stinks.*"

As Mara led the kids out of the classroom, they ran into a flustered-looking Mr. Paine.

"Wait!" the gym teacher called. "I'm meant to be looking after you all while Ms. Abaza deals with a crisis. I'm sorry I got here so late, but I had a crisis of my own. I tripped over a pair of headphones left under the oak tree, and I grazed my knee—"

"Can't stop, Mr. Paine! We have some mice to save!" said Yolanda.

"Wait!" he called out again, but the kids were already running away.

Jeremiah was sure Mr. Paine was going to chase after them, but instead, when he turned to quickly look over his shoulder, he saw Mr. Paine walking into the classroom. "Hey," he heard the teacher say, "what's that buzzing sound?"

The kids followed Mara all the way to the school vegetable garden. She crouched down beside the carrots and pointed.

There was a rainbow-shaped wire mesh structure placed over the top of a big box that had holes punched in it. The holes looked like they might have been made with a pen.

"The mice are in there with some pieces of corn from my lunch salad and some ripped-up paper from my notebook. I also put some wire mesh over them to keep them safe from predators. After I took them, I got worried that they would be vulnerable to mouse-killer cats or birds if I set them completely free. So I googled how to make a mouse house. There were some boxes here, from the seedlings, and wire mesh all around. I made this makeshift house for them until I could figure out a better plan." Mara looked over at Jeremiah sheepishly. "Do you think I did a really bad job of setting the mice free?"

Jeremiah shook his head. "No, I think you are really kind and you did a great job." He lifted the wire and pulled out the box. He opened the box, and everyone looked inside. When they saw that the mice were still happily sleeping in the paper, everyone cheered (very quietly).

"I agree," said Jedda. "It's so cool that you both love animals. Maybe this weekend the three of us could go to a petting zoo. They have Australian animals there. I could teach you all about them!" She winked at Jeremiah. "No bunyips, though."

"I am totally coming too!" said Tom.

"And me!" Yolanda said.

The kids followed Jeremiah, who was carrying the mice in the box, back to the classroom. On the way, they discussed their plans for designing a big, fancy castle for all the mice to live in.

Mara felt happier than she had in a long time. She felt included.

Jedda felt the happiest she had been since arriving in the United States. She felt like she fit in.

Jeremiah was happy too. He felt like people liked him, just for being himself.

Tom felt excited about hanging out with his new friends.

And Yolanda? Yolanda was collecting a bunch of ideas for her game. It was going to be called *Lab Mice Heist*! And the mice would be called Tom, Jeremiah, Jedda, Yolanda, and Mara.

When the friends arrived back at the classroom, Ms. Abaza was waiting for them. She was staring down at her cell phone, tapping away furiously with her thumbs. When she heard the door open, she looked up.

"There you are!" she said, pressing her hands to her chest. The phone dropped to the floor with a clatter. "Oh coconuts," she grumbled. She bent down to pick up her phone.

As she wiped off the phone and checked it for damage, the kids filed into the room and took their seats. All except for Jeremiah, who walked to the front of the class and carefully put the mice, one by one, back into their cage. Ms. Abaza turned around just as he was placing the last mouse into its papery nest. The mice slept through the whole thing.

"Jeremiah?" asked Ms. Abaza. "What's going on? Why were the mice outside of the cage? And why were you all out of class? I arrived here to find Mr. Paine in a bit of a state. I lost my phone yesterday! So clumsy of me. But it had my notes in it about all the adventures I want to take you all on. I have to remember to back this thing up! Anyway, Mr. Paine said you ran away from him. What's going on? Jeremiah?"

Jeremiah took a seat at his desk. He looked around at his classmates and his friends. He looked from Yolanda to Tom to Jedda and, finally, to Mara.

Mara looked a bit nervous again. She raised her eyebrows at Jeremiah hopefully. He gave her a tiny nod, and she let out a long, relieved breath.

"Jeremiah?" Ms. Abaza said again.

Jeremiah smiled at her. If there was one thing he'd learned this morning, it was that honesty was super important, but so was friendship. He was friends with Mara now, and he didn't want her to get in trouble.

"It's really fine," he said to Ms. Abaza. "We were just making a plan for how we're going to build a castle for the mice. I'm going to design it—with Mara's help. She loves animals, just like I do, so I think she'll have some great ideas. Then we'll all build it together. It will be big and beautiful and in the style of the architect Paul Williams, but with our own special Checkerbloom Elementary flair."

Ms. Abaza looked like she would say something, but just then, her phone began to buzz in her hand. And it began to glow. Everyone looked at Jedda, who snorted with laughter.

The laughter spread from kid to kid until everyone in the

classroom was chuckling, giggling, and guffawing, tears streaming from their eyes, hands pressed to their aching ribs. Tom nearly fell off his chair because he was laughing so hard.

"Kids?" Ms. Abaza said. She looked completely flabbergasted. "Please! Tell me what's happened."

"It's okay, Ms. Abaza," Jedda said.

Ms. Abaza raised her eyebrows. She wasn't used to Jedda talking in class. What on earth had gone on while she was away searching for her phone?

"Yeah, Ms. Abaza," said Yolanda. "Don't worry. Everything is totally under control."

"We've got it sorted," added Tom.

"Totally," finished Mara. "Nothing to see here. Everything is a-okay."

"Right," said Ms. Abaza slowly. She slipped her phone into her pocket. "Okay," she said, nodding. Finally, she smiled. "Yes, okay. Jeremiah, we can build that castle. But first, I think we need to name these little guys. Does anyone have any ideas?"

"I do," said Mara. Everyone turned to look at her.

Mara looked over at Jedda. "I think Jedda should name them," she said. "She never got to tell us her ideas. And she's the newest member of our class, and we want her to feel really welcome, don't we?"

She nodded at Jedda, who felt almost teary with happiness.

"As long as you don't call any of them *E.T.*," Mara added in a low voice. She rolled her eyes. "Aliens? What was I even thinking?"

"Nah, aliens are cool!" Tom replied.

"Pop-Tarts for the aliens!" everyone chimed in together.

It started with Jedda, who snorted again. Before long, the whole class was in stitches once more.

Ms. Abaza looked around at her class, still completely bemused, but thinking that something amazing and magical must have happened while she was away. She was sad to have missed it.

She looked into the mouse cage, where the mice were still sleeping. Her brow wrinkled in confusion.

When she looked back up, all of her students were staring back at her, smiling like little angels. She decided in that moment that she would probably never know what had really happened. But that was okay.

"All right, class," she said. "Let's talk about this mouse castle . . ."

About the Author

Kate Gordon grew up in a small town by the sea in Tasmania. Her book *Writing Clementine* received the 2016 IBBY Ena Noël Award. In 2018, Kate was shortlisted for the Dorothy Hewett Award for an Unpublished Manuscript, and she was commended in the 2018 Australian/Vogel's Literary Awards. Kate also has two picture books, two series, and two novels forthcoming.

About the Illustrator

Courtney Huddleston lives in Houston, Texas, with his wife, two daughters, and two cats named Lilo and Stitch. When he's not in his home studio working, he can usually be found playing video games, drooling over the work of other artists, going on long walks, or playing pranks on the family. While he gets inspiration from everything around him, his favorite way to get inspired is through travel. Courtney has been to most of the states in the United States, and he has visited more than a dozen other countries. He is currently searching for less-expensive inspirations.

Check out a sneak peek from...

WHAT HAPPENED?
SANDWICH SHENANIGANS

Chapter 1
MISSING

Monday, May 6, 7:48 a.m.

It was Monday morning. Not just any Monday morning, though. Not for Mr. Hargrove's class, staggering into school with still-wet paintings, dioramas, and not-so-miniature Statues of Liberty for the fifth-grade STEAM project fair. Students lugged around home-sewn patchwork quilts, sequined dance costumes, something that looked suspiciously like a stuffed alligator head peering out from under a dishcloth, and no fewer than three Brooklyn Bridges built from craft sticks. The first two bridges made it all the way to class in perfect condition, but the third looked as if it had fought with Godzilla on the way in . . . and lost. Yes, there was a Godzilla too, an enormous snarling one made of papier-mâché, with a wild look in his painted eyes and a bridge-shaped dent at the end of his scaly nose.

"Your project can be anything you want," Mr. Hargrove had told the students a few weeks earlier, "as long as it follows the theme of this term's topic: What My Country Means to Me. You might want to base it on a special place, a special memory, or a special person. It's entirely up to you. And the good news is that Miss Patterson and I will be working on a project of our own as well—a themed treasure hunt around the school on the morning of the fair, as a reward for all your hard work."

It had been hard work, yes, but fun too. And apart from the poor owner of Craft-Stick Bridge Number Three (who'd disappeared into the stationery cupboard in search of some radioactive-monster-proof glue), the students couldn't have been more pleased with the finished results, proudly showing off their own projects while admiring everyone else's.

"Another Brooklyn Bridge? Snap!"

"I've never seen an alligator up close before. Look at those teeth!"

"Ninety-seven verses? That must be the longest poem about a football game EVER!"

There was no shortage of unique ideas. Jake Parry had made a four-hour film about libraries. Mina Henderson had made a tiny model of her own house inside a matchbox. And Sam Witt . . . well, Sam had made a sandwich. That's right, Sam Witt's finished project was a sandwich. But oh boy, what a sandwich it was.

It was a wonder. A whopper. An eye-boggling, breathtaking, jaw-dropper of a thing. It was America on a plate, with flag-topped burger picks to keep the tomatoes from escaping and a different filling for each state. Yes, Sam Witt's sandwich was a work of art—a triple-quadruple decker built with loaf-sized slices and stuffed with some of the most delicious foods known to man; from pastrami, pickles, and peanut butter to chipotle, chicken, and cheese, with sauces in all the colors of the rainbow.

The other projects were forgotten the moment Sam walked in with his creation, his classmates jostling around his desk for a closer look.

"Holy underpants, Batman," said Ravi, eyes bulging behind his steamed-up glasses, "that's INCREDIBLE! It's a mega-mutant monster!"

"I wish I'd thought of this," said Mateo, licking his lips. "It looks delicious."

"That is one eee-norrrr-mous sandwich," announced Deena in her best funny voice. "That sandwich deserves a place in the—" She stopped short, glancing up at the teacher who'd appeared in the doorway. "Who's that?" she whispered. "And where's Mr. Hargrove?"

"Good morning, students," said the teacher in question, heading for Mr. Hargrove's desk. She was a tall lady with a shock of long red hair and a huge, bulging stomach. She was clearly several months pregnant. "My name is Mrs. Ample, and I'll be teaching your class this morning. If you could leave your projects at the back and find your seats, we'll be ready to begin."

"What happened to Mr. Hargrove?" asked Ravi, wiping his glasses on the front of his T-shirt. "He's supposed to be putting on a treasure hunt for us today. A joint one with Miss Patterson's class."

There was a loud chorus of disappointed groans as the students remembered their last substitute teacher, who'd treated them to a two-hour math test—in silence—followed by an hour of spelling.

"Don't worry," Mrs. Ample assured them. "I understand from Miss Patterson that the treasure hunt is already set up, with more than a hundred fact cards hidden around the school grounds for you to find. Each card covers a different fact about the United States, so you'll be learning as you go. Don't look so anxious," she added. "There's no reason why the hunt can't go ahead as planned once we've taken attendance."

The children's groans turned to cheers, and all thoughts of Mr. Hargrove were forgotten, especially when Mrs. Ample explained that there'd be prizes for the class who found the most cards. This was their class's big chance to beat those boastful show-offs next door! The students ferried their projects to the long table at the back of the room, with Sam Witt's sandwich in pride of place, like a glowing beacon of breaded wonder, then hurried back to their seats for attendance.

"Here."

"Yep."

"Present."

Mrs. Ample ticked them all off one by one (apart from Shaniqua, who would probably be late as usual) and then sent them next door to get their instructions for the treasure hunt. She'd be out to help supervise in a bit, she told them, once she finished getting everything ready for the fair.

WHOOSH!

SCRAM!

CLATTER!

...

Want to read what happens next?

Find out in...

WHAT HAPPENED?

SANDWICH SHENANIGANS

AVAILABLE NOW!